Alma Flor Ada F. Isabel Campoy

Translated by **Joe Hayes and Sharon Franco**

Celebrate
Fourth of July
with Champ, the Scamp

Illustrated by **Gustavo Mazali**

loqueleo

"Let's go on a picnic!" says Mom.

"What will we eat?" asks Leonor.

"I want hot dogs," says Tomás.

"I want hamburgers," says Andrés.

"I only eat chicken," Leonor reminds them.

"I'll make a salad," says Mom.

"That's too much!" Julián complains.
"Don't expect me to carry all that!"

"Let's play baseball," says Andrés.
"Where's the bat?"

"Let's play football," says Tomás.
"Where's the ball?

"Let's play volleyball," says Leonor.
"Where's the net?"

"Where's Champ?
We can't go without Champ!" says Anita.

"Let's not take the dog. He'll run away," warns Julián.
"Don't expect me to chase after him!"

"This basket is so heavy!" says Julián. "But at least we didn't bring Champ."

"There aren't any kids around here," Leonor complains.

"We can't play baseball," Andrés complains.

"Or football, either," Tomás complains.

"And I really miss Champ," complains Anita.
"Let's take a walk. Maybe we'll find someone," suggests Mom.

But poking out of the basket,
what do we see?
The funny little nose
of a dog, sweet as can be.

Help yourselves, my friends!
Here's a tasty treat—
Hot dogs, chicken, hamburgers…
Come on, my friends, and eat!

"Have some of our sushi."

"Here's some falafel and hummus."

"And lots of fried chicken!"

With so many friends,
the children jump and run,
laugh, play, and sing.
They have a lot of fun.

"Even though you're such a scamp,
I really love you, little Champ!" says Anita.

July 4 is the birthday of the United States. Americans have a big party to celebrate the day.

When the United States was formed, there were only 13 states. At first, they were called "colonies" and they were ruled by another country named England.

In 1776, many, many years ago, the 13 colonies decided to break away from England. They explained why in a paper, which was called the "Declaration of Independence." On July 4, 1776, a group of people from the colonies signed the Declaration of Independence.

But England didn't want to let the colonies go. So there was a war between England and the 13 colonies.

The 13 colonies

In the end, the 13 colonies won and decided to form a new country together. They named it the "United States of America." Look how much it's grown since then!

The Fourth of July is also known as Independence Day. It is such an important holiday that most people don't go to work that day. Many people fly the American flag in front of their houses and do something special to celebrate.

Since this is a summer day, most people go outdoors and have lots of fun. Many families go on picnics or have barbecues at home with relatives and friends.

Many cities have parades. The streets are crowded. There are bands, soldiers, firemen, police, old-fashioned cars, horses, and people in costumes. They all go marching by. Every city has its own style of parade.

The big celebration ends with fireworks at night. One of the most famous fireworks shows is in Washington, D.C., the capital of the country. It is amazing!

The Fourth of July is a wonderful day!

Children in Independence Day Parade
© Ariel Skelley/CORBIS

Children in historical costumes in Independence Day Parade, Nevada City, California
© Morton Beebe/CORBIS

Fireworks display over the Statue of Liberty, New York City, New York
© Bettmann/CORBIS

Fire Chief's car in Independence Day Parade, Ojai, California
© Joseph Sohm; ChromoSohm Inc./CORBIS

Detail of signatories from the painting *Declaration of Independence, 4 July, 1776* by John Trumbull, Philadelphia, Pennsylvania
© Bettmann/CORBIS

Marching band in Independence Day Parade, Pacific Palisades, California
© Joseph Sohm; ChromoSohm Inc./CORBIS

Original Declaration of Independence
© Joseph Shom; Visions of America/CORBIS

Independence Day fireworks display over national monuments, Washington, D.C.
© Kevin Fleming/CORBIS

National Guard Officers' residences, St. Augustine, Florida
© William A. Bake/CORBIS

Independence Day fireworks display over the Gateway Arch, St. Louis, Missouri
© Conrad Zobel/CORBIS

Father and child enjoy Grandpa's barbecue
© Ariel Skelley/CORBIS

Independence Day fireworks display at Philadelphia Museum of Art, Philadelphia, Pennsylvania
© Bob Krist/CORBIS

Police officers ride their motorcycles in pyramid formation in Independence Day Parade, Pacific Palisades, California.
© Joseph Sohm; ChromoSohm Inc./CORBIS

Horse riders in the Buffalo Bill Cody Stampede Independence Day Parade, Cody, Wyoming
© Kevin R. Morris/CORBIS

Celebrate and Grow

Throughout history, and in all parts of the world, people get together to celebrate historic anniversaries, commemorate an important person's life, or to ring in a special period of the year. Common to all these celebrations is the acknowledgment that life is a marvelous gift, and that getting together with family and friends makes us happy.

In a multicultural society like that found in the United States, the fact that so many diverse groups live so closely together invites us to know our own culture better, and to discover the cultures of others. Anyone who explores his or her own culture recognizes his or her own identity in the mirror, and affirms his or her sense of belonging to a group. By learning about different cultures, we can observe life as it appears through the windows of those cultures.

This series offers children the opportunity to get closer, for the first time, to the rich cultural landscape of our communities.

The Fourth of July

We have always marveled at the variety of ways in which Americans celebrate their biggest national holiday in every corner of the country.

In Boston, people cover the banks of the Charles River with blankets to enjoy a mid-afternoon concert. In Atlanta, there are parades with period costumes. In Pecos, Texas, the nation's birthday is celebrated with the most important rodeo of the year. Miami's Bayfront Park hosts an exuberant spectacle of music and fireworks. From Malibu, in Southern California, to the shores of Lake Erie, in Cleveland, groups of friends and families spend the day at the beach.

However people celebrate, everyone marks this important day in the history of the United States with great joy.

Alma Flor Ada and F. Isabel Campoy

To Natalia Méndez—may your life always be a celebration.
      FIC & AFA

loqueleo

© This edition:
2018, 2006, Santillana USA Publishing Company, Inc.
2023 NW 84th Ave
Miami, FL 33122
www.santillanausa.com

Text © 2006 Alma Flor Ada and F. Isabel Campoy

Managing Editor: Isabel C. Mendoza
Copyeditor: Eileen Robinson
Art Director: Mónica Candelas

Loqueleo is part of the **Santillana Group**, with offices in the following countries:
ARGENTINA, BOLIVIA, CHILE, COLOMBIA, COSTA RICA, DOMINICAN REPUBLIC, ECUADOR, EL SALVADOR, GUATEMALA, MEXICO, PANAMA, PARAGUAY, PERU, PUERTO RICO, SPAIN, UNITED STATES, URUGUAY, AND VENEZUELA

Celebrate Fourth of July with Champ the Scamp
ISBN: 978-1-68292-567-6

All rights reserved. No part of this book may be reproduced, transmitted, broadcast or stored in an information retrieval system in any form or by any means, graphic, electronic or mechanical, including photocopying, taping and recording, without prior written permission from the publisher.

Published in the United States of America
Printed in USA by Bellak Color, Corp.
22 21 20 19 18   1 2 3 4 5 6 7 8 9

Library of Congress Cataloging-in-Publication Data

Ada, Alma Flor.
    [Celebra el cuatro de julio con Campeón, el glotón. English]
    Celebrate Fourth of July with Champ the Scamp / Alma Flor Ada, F. Isabel Campoy; illustrated by Gustavo Mazali.
    p. cm. — (Stories to celebrate)
    Summary: Champ the dog hitches a ride in the basket for the Fourth of July picnic. Includes nonfiction information about the holiday.
    ISBN 1-59820-131-X
    [1. Dogs—Fiction. 2. Picnicking—Fiction. 3. Fourth of July—Fiction.]
    I. Campoy, F. Isabel. II. Mazali, Gustavo, ill. III. Title. IV. Series.

PZ7.A1857Cel 2005
[E]—dc22   2005031982